Once Upon a PRINCESS and a PEA

Story by
Ann Campbell

Illustrated by
Kathy Osborn Young

STEWART, TABORI & CHANG
NEW YORK

Text copyright © 1993 by Ann J. Campbell
Illustration copyright © 1993 by Kathy Osborn Young
Designed by Paul Zakris

Published in 1993 by
Stewart, Tabori & Chang
575 Broadway, New York, New York 10012

Library of Congress Cataloging-in-Publication
Data

Campbell, Ann.
    Once upon a princess and a pea / story by
Ann Campbell ; illustrated by Kathy Osborn
Young.
        p.   cm.
    Summary: In a modern interpretation of the
classic fairy tale, the independent-minded
Princess Esmerelda proves her royalty by feel-
ing a pea through twenty mattresses.
    ISBN 1-55670-289-2
    [1. Fairy tales.]   I. Young, Kathy Osborn,
ill.   II. Andersen, H. C. (Hans Christian),
1805–1875. Prindsessen paa ærten.   III. Title.
PZ8.C1426On   1993
    [E]—dc20   92-30526

Distributed in the U.S. by Workman
Publishing, 708 Broadway, New York,
New York 10003

Distributed in Canada by Canadian Manda
Group, P.O. Box 920 Station U, Toronto,
Ontario, M8Z 5P9

Distributed in all other territories (except
Central and South America) by Melia
Publishing Services, P.O. Box 1639,
Maidenhead, Berkshire, SL6 6YZ England

Central and South American accounts should
contact Export Sales Manager, Stewart, Tabori
& Chang

Printed in Singapore
10 9 8 7 6 5 4 3 2 1

For Kristina and Robin
—A.J.C.

For Jacob, Lizzy, and Sarah
—K.O.Y.

Princess Esmerelda was beautiful both inside and out, as true princesses sometimes are. She was very well liked, and all the young neighborhood royalty came over to her castle's grounds to play. In the garden was an enormous pool, said to be ten whales long, and a bewildering maze of hedges. When Esmerelda hid there playing hide-and-seek after dark, no one could ever find her.

One day, the princess was summoned to the throne room to see her parents, the king and queen. They were a very proper king and queen and expected their daughter to be a very proper princess. They told Esmerelda that she was soon to be married to King Frobius, a king of great wealth and power. He had a kingdom all his own. They did not mention, however, that King Frobius was fifty-three years old, that dancing was forbidden in his kingdom, or that he had lost almost all of his teeth—which everyone knew, even the lowliest servant.

Esmerelda kept a brave face while her future was discussed, but once she was dismissed she ran to the high wall of battlements that surrounded the castle—her favorite spot for thinking, or for crying, if crying was needed. There the princess stood gazing over the town below, where she could see children playing.

"Why can't I be one of them and not a princess at all?" she sniffled to herself. "Why do I have to be a princess?" Then, she heard another voice inside her answer, "Who said you had to stay a princess? Why not just hightail it out of here before that toothless old king gets his hands on you?"

Princess Esmerelda knew when to take her own advice, as most true princesses do, and she planned her escape. She would leave the castle at night and run whichever way the wind was blowing. She would not be a princess anymore and someone else could marry the toothless king.

That very night, Esmerelda put on all her clothes, one on top of the other, for she did not know what girls who weren't princesses wore. All bundled up, she just barely fit down the winding back staircase and through the iron gate that was a secret entrance to the garden maze. She waddled as fast as she could along the twisted paths until she reached a hidden hole that led out of the maze, into the forest, and to the world beyond. Esmerelda struggled out of the leafy hole, put her finger in her mouth to wet it, then held it up to see which way the wind was blowing. It was blowing from the west, so she ran east. The wind whistled in her ears as she ran, which made her laugh out loud.

Meanwhile, in another kingdom, Prince Hector was also having some family problems. His parents, the king and queen, had told him that he must begin that very day to search for a true princess to be his bride. His mother gave him a handful of hard peas and instructed him to place one beneath the mattress of each princess he met in his travels. If she slept soundly through the night, he would know she was not a true princess.

Prince Hector did not like the princesses he had known
while growing up. They giggled instead of laughed and they
were too scared to play hide-and-seek after dark. Neverthe-
less, Hector jumped in his red roadster and drove off to find
a true princess.

Word of Prince Hector's quest went before him. The king and queen at the first castle had a princess they were eager to see married. They welcomed the prince with open arms and ordered a banquet to be held in his honor.

The princess was to wear red, which was the prince's favorite color. The palace chefs were to cook the prince's favorite foods. And the musicians were to play the prince's favorite song.

That evening, the prince met the princess. She was wearing a regal red dress but, unfortunately, red was not a color that suited her. All the prince's favorite foods had been prepared, but the palace chefs did not know how to cook them and mixed up all the ingredients and recipes. The musicians struck up Prince Hector's favorite song and played it merrily, but they played nothing else all night, until the prince never wanted to hear it again.

The prince asked to be excused early, but before going to bed he managed to sneak into the princess's room and put a pea beneath her mattress, just as his mother had instructed him. The next morning, before he said good-bye, the prince asked the princess whether she had slept well. "Oh, heavens, yes," the princess said, "I slept like a baby." So Prince Hector thanked the king and queen and left without any mention of marriage.

Prince Hector started out toward the next castle, and again word of his journey spread before him: The prince no longer likes his favorite things; he must be in search of great variety.

At the second castle, the king and queen had not one but three princesses looking for husbands. Arrangements were made for a banquet to celebrate the prince's arrival.

That night, Prince Hector met the three princesses. Each princess tried to dazzle him by making sure that she would stand out from the others. Each dressed and behaved so differently that they scarcely seemed like sisters at all. Each had chosen a different menu to be served, confusing Prince Hector so that he did not know what to eat when. Each princess had hired different musicians who played their tunes very well but, unfortunately, all at the same time.

The prince was certainly dazzled. So dazzled, in fact, that he retired early with a headache—but not before placing a pea beneath the mattress of each of the princesses' beds. The next morning, the royal family gathered to see the prince off, hoping that he would take one of the princesses with him. But when he asked each of them how they had slept, the eldest said she had slept marvelously, the middle princess, wonderfully, and the youngest, magnificently. So Prince Hector thanked the king and queen and left without any mention of marriage.

As the prince drove to the next castle, he decided that if he found no true princess there, he would go home without a bride.

Once again word of his journey went before him. The king and queen had heard from the first castle that he did not like his favorite things and from the second castle that he did not appreciate great variety. They made special preparations, hoping the prince would find one of their five princesses right for marriage.

Again, a banquet was held and there the five princesses appeared. Each seemed to be a mirror image of the next. They wore the same white dresses and identical white shoes. They wore the same white flowers in their identical white hair. On a white table were white linens and white vases of white flowers. White food was served on white plates. The musicians played many tunes, but they all played the same white instrument.

Yawning his apologies, the prince went to bed early, but not before slipping a pea under each princess's mattress.

The next morning, the five princesses lined up to see the prince off. "And how did you sleep, uh . . . ," he tried to remember their names, but could not. They had slept soundly. So Prince Hector thanked the king and queen and left without any mention of marriage.

It started to rain as Prince Hector set off. The prince was glad he had decided to go home, even though it meant facing his parents in defeat. His thoughts being very deep and the rain being very hard, Prince Hector almost did not see the figure ahead of him on the road. It looked like a walking bundle of very wet clothes. When the prince caught up to the figure he discovered not just a bundle of wet clothes, but a young woman.

"Where are you going in this rain?" the prince asked in his princely voice.

"Wherever I may find shelter," answered the bundle with a muffled, bundled sort of voice.

The prince offered her a bed at his parents' castle, which she accepted. Along the way, the bundle told her tale, leaving out the fact that she was a princess, or rather that she was no longer a princess. She told the prince that she was supposed to marry an old man with no teeth and that she hated the thought of it, so she had run away. In turn, the prince told the bundle about his troubles finding a true princess to wed, leaving out any mention of his mother's special pea test. They both agreed that true princesses and pleasing husbands were hard to find. It was late by the time they reached the castle, but the king and queen were still up.

"I certainly hope that this bundle of rags is not the princess you plan to marry," declared the queen.

"I would rather wed this bundle of rags, who kept me such good company along the lonely road, than any of the princesses I have met in my travels," said the prince. "If only you were a real princess," he whispered to the bundle.

"But I am a real princess," the bundle whispered back. "At least I was until I ran away."

"Mother! Do you hear that? The bundle is a princess, after all. We can be married immediately."

The queen thought it impossible and absurd that this bundle of wet rags could be a princess. "We shall see how much of a princess she is by tomorrow morning," the queen muttered. "You will stay the night, won't you? I will have a very special bed made up just for you."

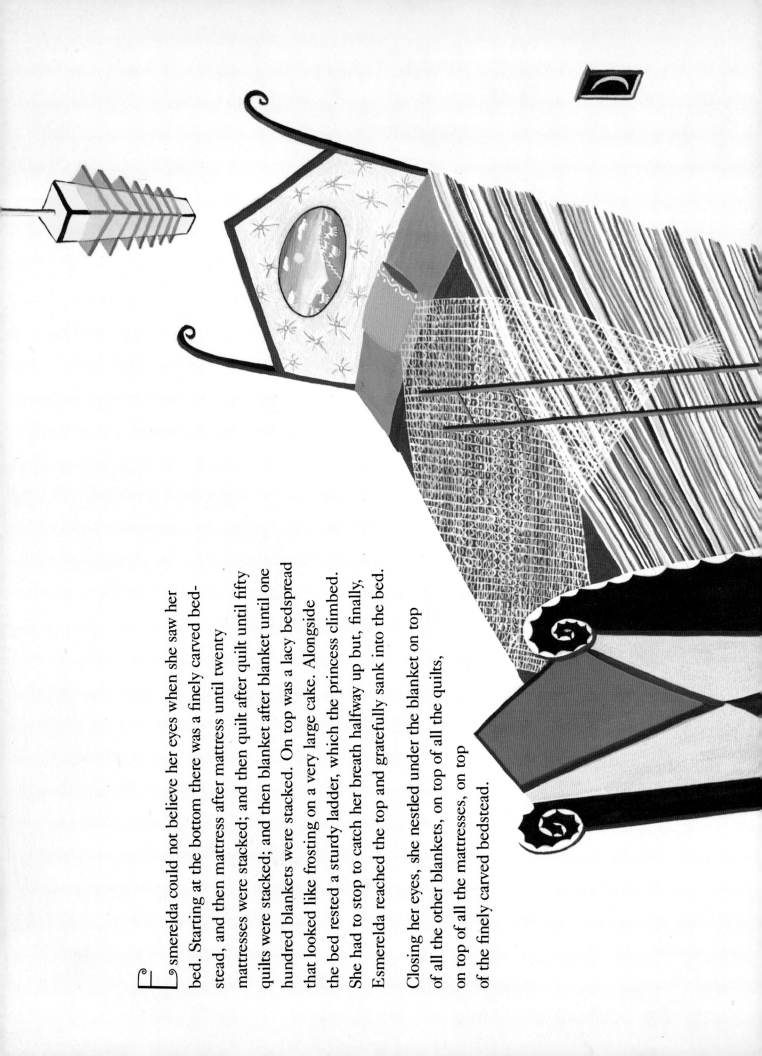

Esmerelda could not believe her eyes when she saw her bed. Starting at the bottom there was a finely carved bedstead, and then mattress after mattress until twenty mattresses were stacked; and then quilt after quilt until fifty quilts were stacked; and then blanket after blanket until one hundred blankets were stacked. On top was a lacy bedspread that looked like frosting on a very large cake. Alongside the bed rested a sturdy ladder, which the princess climbed. She had to stop to catch her breath halfway up but, finally, Esmerelda reached the top and gratefully sank into the bed.

Closing her eyes, she nestled under the blanket on top of all the other blankets, on top of all the quilts, on top of all the mattresses, on top of the finely carved bedstead.

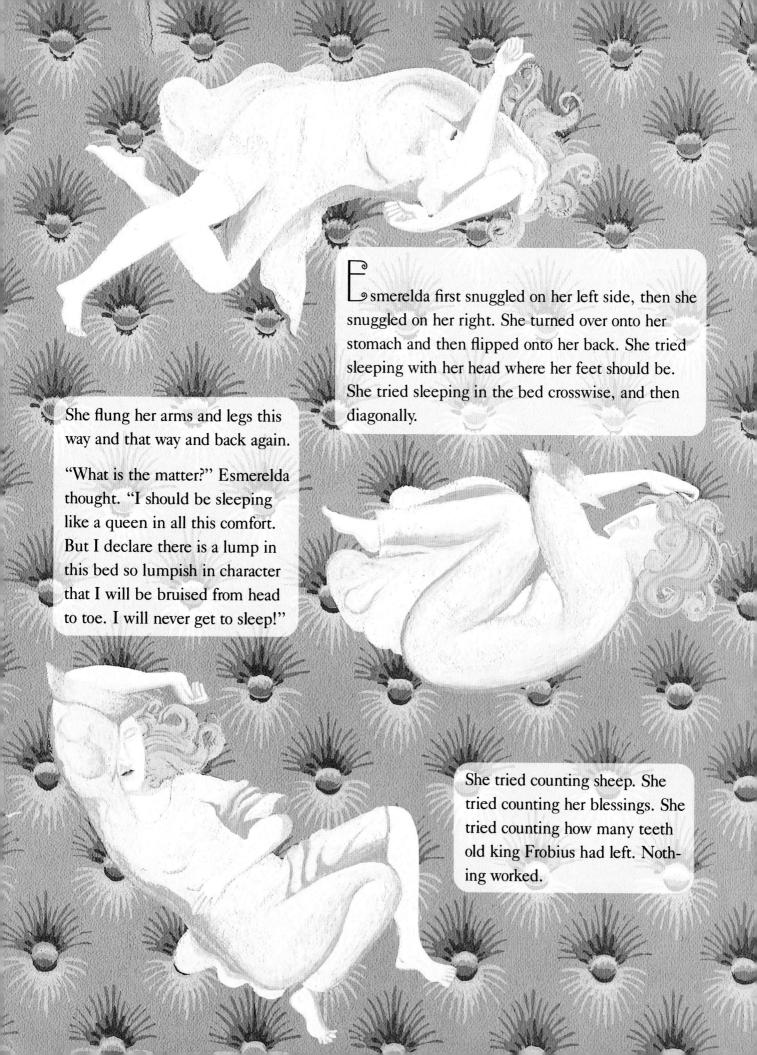

Esmerelda first snuggled on her left side, then she snuggled on her right. She turned over onto her stomach and then flipped onto her back. She tried sleeping with her head where her feet should be. She tried sleeping in the bed crosswise, and then diagonally.

She flung her arms and legs this way and that way and back again.

"What is the matter?" Esmerelda thought. "I should be sleeping like a queen in all this comfort. But I declare there is a lump in this bed so lumpish in character that I will be bruised from head to toe. I will never get to sleep!"

She tried counting sheep. She tried counting her blessings. She tried counting how many teeth old king Frobius had left. Nothing worked.

When dawn finally came, Esmerelda wearily climbed out of bed and down the ladder. She stood before the mirror and moaned to see dark circles under her eyes. Now she would never be able to prove to the queen that she was a princess. Every bone in her body ached. Her skin felt bruised. Her hair was a tousled, tangled mess. She looked most un-princess-like.

Esmerelda put on a bathrobe and crept out of her room. Delicious smells of breakfast wafted toward her and she was so hungry after her running away and her sleepless night that she followed them down the hall, down some stairs, and then down some more stairs, and then down even some more stairs. At the bottom she found herself in the palace kitchen, where the servants were heading toward the dining room with the royal breakfast trays, tureens, teapots, and toast racks. Esmerelda, hungrily breathing in every smell, got in line after the last servant.

The princess followed the parade of servants into the dining room. When the royal family spotted her bringing up the rear, there was quite a commotion.

"So," cried the queen, "you are a kitchen maid after all!"

Before anyone could make any sense out of the situation, Esmerelda said, "I know I look perfectly wretched. I could not sleep a wink last night. I know that on one hundred blankets, on top of fifty quilts, on top of twenty mattresses, all on top of a beautifully carved bedstead, one should sleep very well indeed, but every which way I turned in that bed there was a lump like a stone that kept me from sleeping. If I lay on my right side—the lump was there; if I lay on my left side—the lump was there; the lump was there whether I lay on my back or on my front. I just could not get to sleep. When morning came I was hungry and followed the breakfast smells to the kitchen. And now, because I followed the servants here, you think I am a kitchen maid."

The queen was now smiling. "I beg your forgiveness for a sleepless night and for jumping to conclusions. Here," she proclaimed, "is a true princess. Before making your bed, I placed a hard pea on the bottommost mattress. A mere girl would have taken no notice at all, and would have slept soundly through the night. But how could a true princess sleep with such discomfort? Even if you had politely told a lie and said you had slept well, I should have known you were a true princess by the dark shadows under your eyes and your tousled, tangled hair."

Prince Hector and Princess Esmerelda were happily married. And, the pea? Well, it was put on display in the castle, which is where it is today, unless someone has moved it.